For Liam and Sadie — T. S.

For my little loves: Gabriel, Robbie, Jacob,
Claire, and Sabrene — C. B. S.

Text copyright © 2005 by Tres Seymour
Illustrations copyright © 2005 by Cat Bowman Smith

First edition 2005

Library of Congress Cataloging-in-Publication Data is available.

Library of Congress Catalog Card Number 2004057072

ISBN 0-7636-1242-1

1 2 3 4 5 6 7 8 9 10

Printed in China

This book was typeset in Colwell and Antique Olive.
The illustrations were done in watercolor and ink.

Candlewick Press
2067 Massachusetts Avenue
Cambridge, Massachusetts 02140

visit us at www.candlewick.com

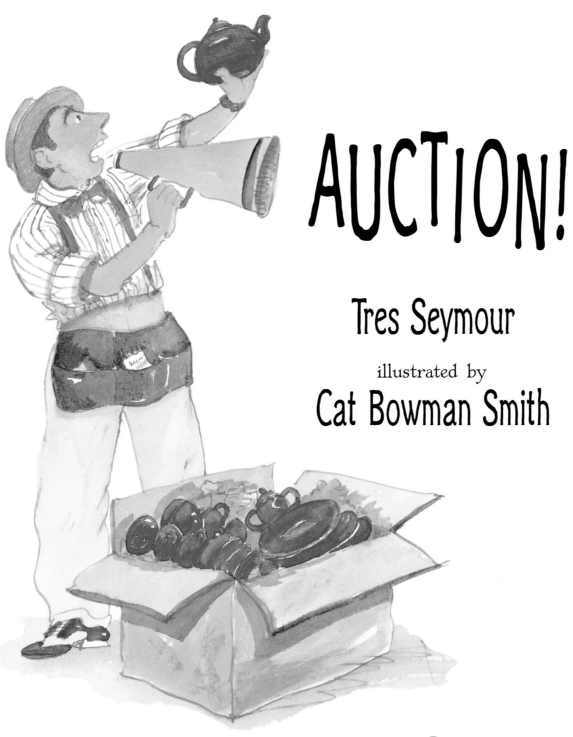

AUCTION!

Tres Seymour

illustrated by
Cat Bowman Smith

CANDLEWICK PRESS
CAMBRIDGE, MASSACHUSETTS

"Whee~oo!

There's going to be an auction!" said Aunt Lou.
Aunt Lou loves an auction better than anything.

"Now Lou, don't get excited," said Uncle Bill.

But it was too late.

Come auction day the whole family—Mama, Daddy,
Uncle Bill, Aunt Lou, my brothers, Homer and Claude Ray,
and me—piled into the truck and drove to the auction.

I brought along the dollar bill I earned helping Daddy
set tobacco. You can't bid at an auction if you don't
have money.

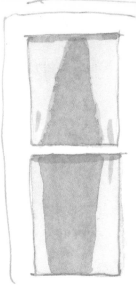

Folks from all over the county were there, deciding what to bid on.

You never saw the like of stuff. There were clothes and glass jars, spoons, quilts, a guitar with no strings, three kerosene lamps, an old saddle, a water barrel, a zinc tub, plastic flowers, a washboard, a big iron potbellied stove, paintings, two toasters, a stuffed groundhog, dishes, a box of springs, marbles, a stack of coat hangers, five umbrellas, a deer's antlers, and a fishbowl.

And that's just what was on top.

I found the only thing
worth anything — a straw hat,
the spitting image of Daddy's.

I tried it on, and it fit me
better than my own hair.

Just then a familiar old car drove up,
and out stepped my teacher, Miss Logsdon.

Miss Logsdon looked at Aunt Lou.

Aunt Lou looked at Miss Logsdon.

Everybody saw that look, and about fifty people gave up right then and went home. Nobody could outbid Aunt Lou and Miss Logsdon when they got going.

The auctioneer, Bubba Philpott, hollered into a bullhorn.

"Ladies and gentlemen, the first lot is a box of old china. We'll start the bidding at two dollars.

Hey!
What am I bid
What am I bid
What am I bid
Do I hear two dollah
two dollah
two dollah
two dollah
who'll give
two dollah?"

"**Two dollars!**" said Aunt Lou.

"**Three!**" said Miss Logsdon right after her.

"**Five!**" said Aunt Lou.

"**Ten!**"

"**Twenty!**"

"**Fifty!**"

"**Seventy!**"

"**Ninety!**" said Miss Logsdon.

Bubba Philpott kept on going.

"The bid is ninety ninety ninety.
Do I hear one hundred?
Hunnerd hunnerd
hunnerd hunnerd
do I hear
one hundred dollah?"

Aunt Lou stamped her foot and said,
"One hundred dollars!"

"One hundred dollars!
Do I hear one ten one ten one ten one ten
won't you go one ten?
Any more? Any more? Once—twice—
and SOLD for one hundred dollars!"

Aunt Lou got the china.
"Oh, mercy," moaned Uncle Bill.

I kept waiting for them to sell the hat. I stood
in front of it, hoping nobody else would see it.
No telling how much it would bring.

My brothers, Homer and Claude Ray, went by,
lugging the old potbellied stove. Who knows what
they'd do with it, since Miss Logsdon and
Aunt Lou didn't want it.

Bubba Philpott kept on and on.

"The next lot is a zinc tub.
I am told it has no holes in it.
I'll start the bidding at three dollars.
Do I hear three dollah three dollah
three dollah three dollah
who'll go three?"

"Three!"
said Miss Logsdon.

"Four!"
said Aunt Lou right after her.

They were off again.

Miss Logsdon got the tub for
a hundred and twenty-five dollars.

"I've got a headache,"
said Uncle Bill.

Everything around that hat sold, one after the other—
the coat hangers, quilts, guitar with no strings, marbles,
box of springs, and the old saddle. Now the hat was
starting to stick out where anybody could see it. Jincey
Jaggers stopped to look at it.

"You don't want that," I told her. "I saw a weevil on it."

Bubba Philpott kept on and on and on.

"What am I bid on this stuffed groundhog?
Let's start the bid at one dollar.
Dollah dollah dollah dollah
who'll give a dollar?
Dollah dollah
dollah dollah—"

"Dollah!"
said Aunt Lou.

"Two dollars!"
said Miss Logsdon.

They were at it again. Aunt Lou got the stuffed groundhog for a hundred and seventy-five dollars.

"I've got to sit down," said Uncle Bill.

Then Bubba Philpott reached over and grabbed up the straw hat. But before he could say a word, Miss Logsdon said, "What a ragged old thing. I wouldn't give you a nickel for it."

"A DIME!" said Aunt Lou.

"A dollar bill!" I hollered.

You could have heard a chicken feather fall in a hay barn. Even Bubba Philpott stuttered to a stop, because nobody ever piped up against Aunt Lou and Miss Logsdon.

At last Bubba Philpott said, **"Any more? Any more? Once — twice —and SOLD for a dollar bill."**

And to this day, I'm the only person who ever outbid
Aunt Lou and Miss Logsdon when they got going.

Aunt Lou says I'm a natural.

Uncle Bill just says he's mighty proud of me.